WHITE EAGLES

ELIZABETH WEIN

Barrington  Stoke

For Mark

First published in 2019 in Great Britain by
Barrington Stoke Ltd
18 Walker Street, Edinburgh, EH3 7LP

www.barringtonstoke.co.uk

Text © 2019 Elizabeth Gatland

A CIP catalogue record for this book is available from the British Library upon request

ISBN: 978-1-78112-896-1

Printed in China by Leo

CONTENTS

PART 1: *Invasion*   1

PART 2: *Escape*   39

PART 3: *Exile*   83

EUROPE 1939

Kristina's journey from
Warsaw to Swanage

GREAT
BRITAIN

Swanage

Cherbourg

FRANCE

Nantes

Bergerac

Alto

Montpellier

PART 1: *Invasion*

CHAPTER 1

"I can't believe you've been called up first!"
Leopold said as he stared at the letter his twin
sister Kristina had just opened. "Unfair!"

Leopold stood by the hall table at the bottom of
the stairwell – where all the post for their building
got left. Kristina's letter was headed with the
Polish Air Force's crest – a fierce white eagle.

Last year, Kristina and Leopold Tomiak had
both completed their basic pilot training. Now
they shared a flat and worked as instructors at
the Vistula Aeroclub outside Warsaw. It was the
summer of 1939 and three months until their
nineteenth birthday.

It had been an uneasy summer – Germany's
army was gathering near Poland's borders. All of
Europe was worried. The German Luftwaffe was
the most fearsome air force in the world. Every
now and then you could see their spy planes flying
high over Warsaw. It made your skin crawl when

you looked up, wondering if they'd drop a bomb or fly away without causing trouble.

So far, they'd always flown away.

Kristina and Leopold had signed up for the Polish Air Force Reserve. Now the shadow of war loomed and this letter commanded Kristina to join them. She would be a liaison pilot – flying missions to take strategic photographs, deliver messages and sometimes transport important passengers.

"Why you and not me?" Leopold cried. Kristina's brother was hot-headed and open-hearted, always bad at hiding his emotions. "I got my pilot's licence first!" he added. "And I've trained more solo flyers than you have!"

Kristina laughed. She was the more level-headed of the twins and was used to Leopold's dramatics. "You only just edged ahead of me this morning!" she reminded him. "I was winning yesterday, before your solo student today. And tomorrow I'll be in the Air Force!"

"I expect my letter has been delayed in the post," Leopold said. "What kind of missions do they want you to fly?" He snatched the letter from Kristina's hand so he could see it better. "Communications. You'll still be based at the

Vistula Aeroclub. Oh, and the plane they're giving you is just an RWD-8. A training aircraft – like we fly every day!"

"It has an extra fuel tank," Kristina pointed out. "It can go twice as far as those old flight-school trainers. I'll be leaving you in the dust."

She turned to meet her brother's eyes. She could tell by the look on Leopold's face that he was proud of her – if also a bit envious.

Kristina knew they'd probably be sent to different regiments at some point, but she hoped they wouldn't be too far away from each other for now. Leopold was her best friend as well as her brother – they'd moved away from home together and were so busy with work that they hardly saw their parents.

"Kristina Tomiak, fearless scout for the Polish Air Force!" Leopold said. "A young eagle! You'll be spying on German troops – leading fighter pilots to their prey! Perhaps they're giving the liaison jobs to the girls so that the men can fly the fighter planes. No doubt they'll make me a fighter pilot when I get my letter."

"If no one tips them off about how big-headed you are," Kristina told him.

"Hah." Leopold laughed. "Then you'll be jealous of me instead of the other way round!"

Kristina thought he was probably right about the women pilots getting liaison work so that the young men were free to fight. But this letter meant she had real air work to do, and she wasn't jealous at all.

"We'll be eagles together," Kristina said.

CHAPTER 2

Almost a month later, Kristina watched a small plane arriving at the Vistula Aeroclub.

As she squinted into the late-August sun, she saw it was an RWD-8 like hers, with one high wing and two open cockpits. Leopold stood by her side, shielding his eyes with one hand. He hadn't got his call-up letter yet. Since Kristina had joined the Air Force, she had mostly been flying important officials across Poland as the country scrambled to prepare for war with Germany. Leopold always seemed to be around when Kristina set off on a mission.

Kristina was expecting this RWD-8 plane, but she wasn't sure who the passenger was. She just knew he'd been doing dangerous intelligence work in Germany. He'd been picked up in secret from there and was now being passed on to Kristina. She would take him to a meeting in the big southern Polish city of Lvov.

The plane weaved left and right across the blue summer sky. It was buffeted by the wind and looked as fragile as a kite as it sank lower and lower.

"What's wrong with that pilot?" Kristina wondered aloud. "He can't fly in a straight line! How did he ever find his way here from Germany?"

"Perhaps he's working at his skywriting," Leopold said.

Kristina laughed. The best thing about Leopold was that he always saw the sunny side of every situation, up until the very last second.

It could also sometimes be the worst thing about him.

The small plane was close now, very low, coming in just over the end of the airfield. The pilot steadied the wings at last and kept them stable as he floated in to land.

Kristina held her breath as the plane's wheels touched down on the airfield grass. They bounced back up in the air for a moment and then landed again with a thud. It was a hard and uneven landing, and not what she would have expected from a confident Air Force liaison pilot.

"Ouch," Leopold said. "His passenger will be glad to have *you* at the controls for the next leg of the trip, won't he?"

Kristina beckoned to her brother by jerking her head. "Come on, I want to meet them at the hangar when they get there. I already made sure my plane is full of fuel. I'm going to need that extra tank to make it to Lvov in one hop."

They crossed the airfield together. Leopold, good-natured as always, waved as the plane taxied towards the Vistula Aeroclub hangar. Kristina could just see the tops of the heads of the pilot and passenger, in helmets and goggles, peeping out above the edge of the open cockpits.

As they got closer to the plane, Kristina saw there was something wrong with its wing. The thin fabric that covered its wooden frame was torn in the back, and trailing shreds of cloth were fluttering behind the plane in the wind from the propeller.

Then she saw a line of holes peppering the side of the plane below the cockpit.

Someone had been firing at the plane with a machine gun.

As the pilot switched off the aircraft's engine, Leopold leaped forwards ahead of his sister. He jumped up onto the wing strut lightly and leaned in to the cockpit.

"What happened?" Leopold asked.

Kristina couldn't hear the pilot's answer. But she saw him hold up one hand. Blood ran between the pilot's fingers, bright red and dripping. The sleeve of his flight suit was torn and sodden with blood.

One of the bullets that had pierced the aircraft had struck the pilot's arm. That was why his landing had been so unsteady.

Kristina felt as if a jolt of electricity had struck her in the stomach.

The same thing could happen to me, she thought. *He is doing exactly the same job as me, in the same kind of plane.*

The wounded pilot jerked his bloody hand back towards his passenger behind him. Leopold jumped down from the wing strut so he could lean in to talk to the passenger ... and then turned around to look at Kristina with a face as white as a ghost.

"The passenger's dead," Leopold said.

CHAPTER 3

"They came out of nowhere," the pilot said.
"Luftwaffe planes, three of them." He pulled off
his goggles slowly with his good hand. He was
trembling as he climbed out of the plane. "They
had black crosses and swastikas on their tails –
new German fighter planes, the fastest things
I've ever seen ..."

The pilot didn't look much older than Kristina
and Leopold – a thin young man with mousy hair
and intense dark eyes.

"The Luftwaffe were scouting over the city," the
injured pilot said. "And got me just as they were
leaving. I think they were running low on fuel,
because they didn't stick around to finish me off.
The three of them just roared away together as if
they'd decided one weaponless RWD-8 was a waste
of their time."

The scrawny young pilot looked as if he hardly
had the strength to stand. Kristina and Leopold

held him up on each side, taking care not to touch his bleeding arm.

The wounded pilot whispered something as they held him close between them.

"My passenger passed his information on to me before ..." The pilot drew in a deep breath. "Before ... before he died. He wanted me to pass it on to his contact in Lvov, if I can get there."

Two of the Vistula Aeroclub's mechanics were wheeling Kristina's RWD-8 out of the hangar to get it ready for her flight. The mechanics in greasy overalls stared at the still head of the dead passenger slumped in the rear cockpit of the liaison plane. Then they turned to the bleeding pilot between Kristina and Leopold.

"What's going on?" one of the mechanics asked.

Just then, Kristina's commanding officer came racing out of the clubhouse opposite the hangar. He ran straight across the neat, bright flowerbed full of marigolds and geraniums that bordered the lawn in front of the clubhouse.

"Tomiak," the officer barked, and pointed to Leopold. "You're on active duty as of this very minute, along with flight instructors Lipowiski and

Novak. The Air Force regiments are being split up to support the ground brigades, and our orders are to ferry all our P-11 fighter planes away from Warsaw. The Luftwaffe are getting bolder and clearly planning an attack any day. We won't be able to fight the Nazis in the air if they destroy our aircraft on the ground."

Leopold looked stunned. Kristina knew he wanted to be on active duty. But he wanted to fly planes into battle, not ferry them away from the action.

"We're going to move supplies, fuel and ammunition to Lvov, in the south," the commander said. "It's not a strategic or industrial town, so we're hoping the Germans won't target it. Our troops will be able to pick up supplies from Lvov on their way to the Romanian border. The plan is to hold out in Romania until we get support from our British and French allies."

"Sir, am I to go ahead with my mission?" Kristina asked. "The passenger has died, but the pilot has been given his information to pass on."

The commanding officer turned to Kristina and said, "Go ahead. You can take the pilot to our new base, about ten miles outside Lvov, and his contact can meet him there. We'll be in a village called Birky, near the forest. There's an airstrip ready for us there."

The wounded pilot suddenly went limp, sagging as Kristina and Leopold tried to support him. He'd fainted. Kristina felt as if she and her brother were carrying several large sacks of potatoes between them.

"Perhaps we'd better get this fellow to a medic before he goes anywhere," Leopold said gravely. And then, with one last attempt at humour, Leopold added, "Otherwise my sister will need help getting her passenger into her plane."

CHAPTER 4

In the air, Kristina was all right. She was amazed, and pleased, that the wounded pilot in the passenger cockpit behind her was sleeping. Waiting for a doctor had delayed their take-off, and it was a long flight.

So far, Kristina hadn't run into any German planes. After a while, she managed to calm the fluttering feeling in her stomach. She carried on a conversation with Leopold in her head.

I'm such a smooth pilot that my passenger is sleeping like a baby!

She tried to imagine Leopold's response. *Smooth? I'll bet he's sleeping so well because you're rocking the wings like a cradle.*

She couldn't help smiling to herself. That was *exactly* the kind of thing he'd say.

She prayed that Leopold didn't run into any German planes either. He didn't have any combat training, and the fighter plane he was ferrying probably wasn't loaded with ammunition.

Eagles without talons, Kristina imagined Leopold saying.

She arrived at the Birky airstrip outside the city of Lvov and found everyone there preparing for invasion – just the same as in Warsaw. The small airfield was confusingly busy. There were several P-11 fighter planes there already, like the one Leopold was flying. The P-11s seemed much mightier and faster than Kristina's RWD-8, but she knew that they were old-fashioned and no match for the Luftwaffe.

Hey, Leopold, you're quite the Air Force eagle now that you're flying a P-11! Kristina told her twin brother in her head.

Air Force eagle yourself, he replied in her imagination. *Don't forget to deliver your wounded passenger and his intelligence message.*

Kristina taxied her plane close to one of the hangars. Several other pilots and two ground crew came to help Kristina's passenger out of the plane. They seemed to know what was going on. Eventually the wounded pilot was taken away in a car with a man wearing an officer's uniform, and Kristina never saw him again.

It wasn't clear to Kristina where to park her small plane, so she taxied it as far out of the way as possible, to where the airfield bordered a patch of woodland. She found a couple of stones to wedge her RWD-8's wheels so the plane wouldn't roll anywhere.

It seemed like a long hike back to the hangars and sheds that were being used as barracks and offices. Kristina saw a few young women her age wearing flying club instructors' uniforms, just like she had worn until recently. They looked at her Air Force liaison pilot's uniform and white eagle badge with respect.

Leopold had left the Vistula Aeroclub still wearing his instructor's uniform too. He didn't even have an Air Force pilot's badge yet.

When are you going to get a proper kit like mine? she teased Leopold in her head.

"Kristina! Over here!" a voice called out.

She spotted Leopold's dark, handsome head over the top of a dozen other pilots and ran to meet him. They kissed each other's cheeks – one, two, three – and hugged each other.

"You made it to Birky!" Kristina said. "How did you find me?"

"Easy! I knew you'd be the only girl here in proper kit," Leopold said.

Kristina laughed.

"Actually, I was watching for your plane," Leopold explained. "There aren't very many RWD-8s here – they're not worth saving from the Luftwaffe bombs. And I saw the fuss they made over your passenger when you landed."

Kristina linked arms with her brother and they smiled at each other, glad to be together again.

"It's true your kit makes you stand out," Leopold added. "I wish I looked as smart as you. Or had my badge."

Kristina unhooked the silver eagle from above her breast pocket. Its wings flared as it hovered to dive and it carried a victory wreath in its mouth.

"I've got a uniform," Kristina said. "You can have my badge." She pressed it into his hand.

CHAPTER 5

Kristina slept with the other female pilots on folding camp beds in a corner of a mechanics' shed. There were no blankets. Kristina lay with her head on the canvas flight bag that contained her maps and leather helmet. She was determined to try to sleep. She could hear a distant rumble that might have been explosions or maybe just the movement of armed vehicles.

Kristina woke at five o'clock in the morning to the sound of sirens.

It was 1 September 1939. An officer shouted an announcement: fifteen minutes earlier, the German Army had stormed across Poland's northern and western borders, assisted by the Slovakian Army in the south. They were now moving as fast as lightning across Poland, with all their fire and fury aimed at Warsaw.

"Combat training!" said Leopold as he and Kristina drank coffee together hastily. "I'm going to be a student pilot again! The best way to learn something is to do it, right? Off to school!"

Leopold gave Kristina three quick kisses on her cheeks and added, "We'll compare notes at the end of the school day, all right? *Stay safe.*"

They both knew that Kristina's job in the air was just as dangerous as her brother's – maybe *more* dangerous because her plane was slower and wasn't armed. But the Tomiak twins managed to make it back alive each day during that first week of war.

Not much food reached Birky. The transport routes were a mess as soldiers fought and normal people tried to get out of their way. But Kristina could land her RWD-8 in a farmer's field without any trouble and was able to scrounge bread and cabbages and apples between missions. Once she even brought back a vodka bottle full of milk. At the airfield, one of the mechanics kept a fire going in an oil drum to bake potatoes, handing them out to any pilot who stopped by. Kristina and Leopold tried to meet at this makeshift cafe each day at sunset.

"How's school?" Leopold asked his sister. He always seemed cheerful, despite their desperate situation, but today he seemed truly radiant – as if he were nursing a wonderful secret. "Learn anything new today?"

The war had been raging for one week, but it felt like months since they'd left home.

"I learn something new every day," Kristina said. "All of it horrible."

She wondered why Leopold looked so marvellously happy.

It was already clear that the Polish forces were disorganised and badly supplied. They couldn't stand up to their enemy. Britain and France had promised to come to Poland's aid but had done nothing. The capital city of Warsaw was being bombed to pieces. The telephone lines were down, and Kristina's communications work was vital – but that morning she'd narrowly avoided being hit by a volley of Polish anti-aircraft guns. The idiots had taken her for a Luftwaffe bomber while she was delivering a message to another brigade.

"You go first," Kristina said to Leopold as they stood by the oil-drum cafe. "You've clearly got something to tell me that will cheer me up."

Leopold flushed pink with pride. "I shot down a Luftwaffe bomber today," he said.

Kristina gave a wordless cry of fierce delight. Then she asked, "*How?* Aren't they all newer and faster than anything we fly?"

"They can't dive as fast as a P-11 without their wings breaking off," Leopold said. "You have to get overhead when they're not expecting you and dive at them like a hawk going after a mouse—"

"Like an *eagle*, you fool!" Kristina teased.

"Like an eagle. Of course an eagle!" Leopold agreed. He wolfed down his potato, eating it like an apple, without bothering to peel it. Tearing down the sky at six hundred kilometres an hour after enemy aircraft had given him an appetite.

"Your turn," Leopold said. "What have you learned today?"

Kristina tried to make her answer positive.

"We haven't run out of fuel yet." She winced. "That's the best I can do. All the trains and supply lorries are being blown up by German planes."

Leopold nodded. He knew it; he'd seen it from the air.

"The plans are changing all the time," Kristina added. "The latest is that Lvov is supposed to get ready for a heavy attack."

Lvov, only ten kilometres from Birky, had been chosen as a safe place to keep supplies because it was a university city, not an industrial one. But that didn't seem to make the faintest difference to the German Army. Hitler was set on wiping out anything and everything of value in Poland, and on grabbing Polish land. Even the weather seemed to be on his side, the constant clear skies letting the Luftwaffe roam wherever they wanted.

"All the troops are supposed to meet here to stock up on supplies to take to Romania," Kristina reminded her brother. "And the British and the French will back us up. People are starting to build defences around Lvov. We have to get to work to do the same out here at Birky."

She gave Leopold the blackened outer skin of her potato. She'd managed to get him to eat her potato skins for as long as she could remember. It vanished in an instant.

"Well, if we're defending Lvov, we won't have to fly as far," Leopold said, licking his fingers as if burnt potato skins were his favourite food. "And when we have to retreat, we can send Mum and Dad a postcard from Romania!"

It sounded so silly – as if the entire Polish Army retreating to Romania were a Scouts camping trip. Better send Mum a postcard!

But Leopold knew it wasn't funny really. He put his arm around Kristina so that they could huddle close together as they headed for their camp beds.

"Stay safe," Leopold told her as they parted.

CHAPTER 6

That Friday afternoon, smoke began to rise from the village of Birky. It wouldn't be long before the Nazis reached the airfield.

It was fifteen days after the invasion of Poland, and just three fighter planes were still stationed at Birky, including Leopold's. Kristina's sturdy, reliable RWD-8 was their one last liaison plane, but Kristina had spent the past few days on the ground, helping with the frantic work to dig defensive trenches around the airstrip. The German Army was so close that the defences felt almost pointless. Lvov was already being bombarded; you could see the smoke in the sky as the city burned.

And still the sun shone, giving the Nazis the advantage of clear skies and dry roads. Two weeks ago, the Polish Air Force had five hundred planes. Now there were fewer than a hundred left.

Leopold was maddeningly cheerful about still being able to fly. He seemed unconcerned that Lvov was under siege, that the airfield was surrounded by enemy soldiers, and that he was about to be evacuated to Romania.

Leopold was in the air early on Saturday morning when the Germans attacked the small Polish airstrip next to the village of Birky. The German Army was overwhelming, travelling in countless armed lorries, and the half-trained Polish soldiers and Air Force pilots without planes were far outnumbered. The German troops in dull green uniforms stormed their weak defences and filled the air with furious rifle fire.

Kristina sheltered behind the oil drum that had been used for baking potatoes. She had a pistol that her commanding officer had given her for her liaison flights, but it was no good against heavy rifle fire.

The battle for the airfield at Birky was over in less than twenty minutes. The German soldiers swept across the field and into the buildings, gathering prisoners. Behind the oil drum, Kristina found herself staring up the barrel of a German rifle.

"*Aufstehen!*" the soldier ordered. *Get up!* His helmet shadowed his eyes. Kristina couldn't tell how old he was. His expression was neutral, not angry. He barked another order at Kristina, but this one she couldn't understand.

The German soldier was standing right in front of Kristina. With her body half hidden, he didn't see her pistol. She could have shot him.

But there were a dozen other soldiers in the same green helmets standing behind him, all holding rifles like his. Kristina knew that shooting one of them would only lead to her own swift execution. If she did as she was told now, she might get a chance to make a run for it later. She put her pistol in the pocket of her tunic before she stood up. Then she held up her empty hands as she stepped out from behind the oil drum.

The soldier who'd found her moved his rifle to indicate that she should walk in front of him. Kristina didn't argue. A crowd of people she recognised were on the dry, dusty grass of the airstrip – mechanics, soldiers, officers and a few other pilots. One or two of them were bleeding as they stood in untidy rows. Everyone looked grim and stunned. Someone caught Kristina's eye and held her gaze for a moment, then looked away.

What will Leopold find here when he returns from his flight? Kristina thought.

She wondered if the Germans were just going to line everybody up and shoot them. She knew they'd done that in other places.

Suddenly the roar of aeroplanes interrupted the silence. Both the soldiers and prisoners looked up at the sky.

Two fighter planes screamed over the airfield, one German and one Polish.

They came racing after each other, almost as if they were flying in formation at an air show. All the people on the ground craned their necks at the same time to see, as if they were watching a tennis match.

As she saw the fighter planes lined up in the sky together, Kristina understood why the Polish Air Force hadn't stood a chance against the Luftwaffe. The open cockpit of the Polish P-11 made the plane look like an antique. The German Messerschmitt seemed a thousand times more deadly, with its low, blade-like wings and sleek, streamlined body.

But the planes weren't firing at each other.

The fighters sped low over the airfield and wheeled skyward again, and Kristina worked out what was going on. The planes were both out of ammunition, and the German pilot was also running out of fuel. He was trying to land. The Polish plane was hard on his tail and turned sharply to cut off his landing path.

And as the Polish plane flashed past Kristina, she saw its number. It was Leopold's plane.

CHAPTER 7

The German pilot curved around to try to land again. He was taking his time, lining up with the airfield – he knew that the Polish plane behind him couldn't shoot him down.

Leopold didn't follow the German pilot around this time. Instead, he climbed into the sky. He spiralled up higher until his plane looked like a toy silhouette against the blue.

As the German plane came in on its landing path, Leopold plunged down at it like an eagle diving at a hare.

Kristina thought she was about to see her twin brother's plane go up in a ball of flame in the middle of the sky.

Her heart thundered in time with the aircraft engines. They were so loud that Kristina didn't hear the impact as the two planes met overhead.

There was no ball of flame. Instead, just like an eagle, Leopold pulled up gently out of his calculated dive.

He'd somehow managed to hit the tail of the German aircraft with the propeller of his own plane. Leopold must have destroyed his propeller in the impact, but his plane was still in one piece. He straightened its wings and glided calmly overhead, passing above the staring soldiers and prisoners.

The German fighter plane was not so lucky.

Leopold's propeller had sliced its tail off, which had sent the Luftwaffe fighter into a plunging spin. Without the tail section, the German pilot couldn't control his plane. It plummeted out of the sky and hit the airfield so hard and fast that it buried itself in the earth up to its wings.

Still there was no explosion. But in the half-buried plane, crumpled like a sheet of paper, the German pilot must have been killed instantly.

The Polish prisoners let out a roar of triumph. The German soldiers kicked people up and down the crowded lines, whacking them with rifle butts. It didn't take them long to restore order. But the prisoners' feeling of stunned defeat seemed to lift.

Kristina could hear people whispering behind her. Everyone's eyes were still on the sky – on the plane that was miraculously still flying, and on Leopold, who was miraculously *still alive*.

Leopold's plane cut through the sky in silence. He must have shut down his engine after he lost the propeller, to avoid a fire. He made an elegant turn at the other end of the airfield and landed smoothly, near the wreckage of the German plane he'd knocked out of the sky.

Leopold pushed up to sit on the side of his open cockpit above the wing. There was another roar of excitement as he climbed out of the plane. People surged forwards to welcome Leopold and also to shout warnings.

"The Germans are here!" the prisoners yelled. "They've burned the village at Birky! We are being held—"

Leopold's face was glowing, flushed with success and adrenaline. He pushed back his goggles and flight helmet, grinning in spite of the warnings, and swung lightly down from the cockpit of the P-11. The silver wings of the eagle badge that Kristina had given him glinted for a moment in the sunlight.

"Look out—" someone shouted.

Even if the warning had come earlier, Kristina didn't think there was anything Leopold could have done about it.

Leopold reached for his pistol, but not fast enough. Two of the German soldiers grabbed him by the arms and a third hit him hard across the face as Leopold struggled. He staggered for a moment, sagging against the grasp of the soldiers.

The crowd parted suddenly as a German officer swept forwards. The soldiers pushed people aside to make a path. The officer wore a grey uniform with shining black boots. A jagged double S, like a pair of crooked lightning bolts, was embroidered on the officer's collar. His face was utterly blank, as if he felt no human emotion.

Leopold straightened up to face the SS officer as he stopped in front of him. In one swift, calm movement, the officer pulled out a narrow black Luger pistol, pressed it between Leopold's eyebrows and shot him in the head.

CHAPTER 8

The soldiers let go of Leopold's arms. His body fell back against the plane. Behind him, the cockpit windscreen was speckled red with spattered blood.

Kristina fell too, gasping, and for a few moments was unable to breathe. She knelt in the dust of the airstrip, choking on air.

Seconds later, Kristina became aware that the prisoners around her had gone berserk. The execution of Leopold hadn't taught them a lesson – it had whipped them to desperation. They might have been unarmed and outnumbered four to one, but they began a brief, frantic riot of revenge. People ran around Kristina, fighting the German soldiers with their feet and empty hands. She heard guns being fired not far away, the sound thundering in her ears. Someone jumped over Kristina's back as if he were playing at leaping goats in a school playground.

Kristina sucked in air. Behind closed eyes, she saw again the moment of her twin brother's murder.

Why did you land here? WHY? Kristina shouted at Leopold in her head. *You must have seen the village on fire! You must have seen the Nazi lorries and soldiers!*

But maybe the only thing Leopold had been looking at was the Luftwaffe fighter plane ahead of him in the sky. And after he'd attacked, he couldn't have flown anywhere else – he'd lost his propeller.

If only he'd landed further away – by the treeline of the forest – maybe he could have run. He could have *run* ...

Run, Leopold's voice repeated in Kristina's head. *Run.*

Kristina scrambled to her feet. She was still half blinded by tears and grief, but she was no longer frozen. She could think and move.

She ran.

She'd been on the edge of the crowd, and Kristina dodged between the German soldiers in the chaos of her comrades' last violent, hopeless battle. In a moment or two she'd managed to get herself clear of the struggle. Kristina's RWD-8 liaison plane was still standing by itself near the trees at the edge of the airfield. One of the fuel tanks was still full, Kristina knew – she'd checked it herself after her last flight.

She ran for her plane.

Guns rattled behind her. Kristina didn't know if they were firing at her or at someone else, and she wasn't going to waste time looking back to find out. They'd get her or they wouldn't, and there was nothing she could do about it.

She ran.

When she reached the small RWD-8, Kristina yanked the wedges out from under the wheels. She used all her strength to throw the propeller around to start the engine. Then she hauled herself up over the side of the plane and tumbled into the cockpit. She took off recklessly, without even a look at the flight instruments to make sure they were working.

There wasn't any time now for following the normal rules. The only thing that kept Kristina from squeezing the controls in a death-grip was her hundreds of hours of flight experience. She turned the plane to get the wind behind her, and it took her away from the airfield, eastwards out over the forest and towards the rising sun.

Kristina wasn't wearing a flying helmet or goggles. The noise of the RWD-8's engine was deafening, and she had to squint in the propeller's wind. After a few minutes, the city of Lvov came into sight. Smoke and flames rose from where it had already been attacked. Kristina was flying in the wrong direction. If she wanted to escape, she needed to head south or west.

Stay safe! You're too close to the trees. Climb a bit higher. Don't fly into the sun.

Kristina couldn't separate Leopold's voice in her head from her own thoughts. The conversation went on as if nothing had happened to him.

She turned slowly until she faced away from the sun. Her eyes watered and the tears dried instantly in the wind. If anyone was shooting at her from the ground, or chasing after her in the air, she couldn't hear them or see them.

Still in shock, Kristina climbed higher, putting a bigger cushion of air between herself and the ground. But she didn't want to risk going too high in case a powerful Luftwaffe fighter saw her and she wouldn't be able to outfly it. Being close to the treetops kept her camouflaged.

For the next quarter of an hour, all Kristina did was fly away from her twin brother's brutal murder. She was aware of nothing but the sun and wind and air and sky. Her hands and feet moved automatically to keep the plane aloft, as if she were a puppet.

Kristina had no idea where she was. Her compass told her she was flying south. She'd left behind the smoke of Lvov, and she didn't have a map. If she landed anywhere in Poland, she risked facing the same fate as Leopold.

Kristina had no choice: she'd fly until she found a safe place to think and rest, or until she ran out of fuel.

Kristina held her course and kept flying.

PART 2: *Escape*

CHAPTER 9

Kristina thought she'd been flying for an hour, more or less. She chose a narrow field to land in at the edge of an orchard. It was hardly more than a green lane of grass between a line of old apple trees and a dense birch wood. She guessed there must be a farm or cottage or even a village somewhere nearby, but Kristina hadn't been able to spot it. That was a good thing – maybe then no one would notice one little runaway Polish plane sneaking back to the ground. Kristina lined up over the orchard, prayed that there weren't hidden rocks or stumps or apple baskets lying in the grass and gently glided to the ground.

She landed with a soft thump, and the RWD-8 rolled to a stop in the long grass. Kristina cut the power and let the engine die.

She sat in the cockpit with her face leaning on her arms. She took this moment of cool silence to play over in her head the end of her twin brother's life. Leopold's bright face, flushed pink with success and pride as his comrades roared their thanks. The way Leopold had swung down from the cockpit of the P-11 fighter with such easy confidence. The brutal SS officer and the sudden gunshot ...

And the terrible speed of that shot. Leopold might not even have had time to realise what was about to happen to him.

At least it was painless, Kristina told herself. *At least it was fast.*

But she got no comfort from that thought.

Now she was nagged by the practical demands of her aircraft. Kristina knew she needed to check to make sure the plane's undercarriage and control surfaces hadn't been harmed in her hasty take-off. Ripe apples from the nearby trees could keep her going for the rest of the day. It meant she could check the plane, eat and rest, and then try to get some sleep. She didn't think she had the strength to take off again before tomorrow morning.

Kristina raised her head from her arms and straightened up.

The back of her head met a point of hard metal with a bang. For half a second, Kristina thought it was some rod or strut in the aircraft's structure that had come loose and hit her.

Then a gruff voice said, "Put your hands up."

Kristina realised that someone in the cockpit behind her was holding a gun to her head.

Kristina knew that no one could have climbed into the plane since she'd landed. The armed soldier must have been there all along.

One of the Nazi soldiers must have climbed into the plane right behind her at Birky. He had hidden in the rear cockpit and kept his head down during her entire getaway flight. He only dared to confront her now they were safely on the ground.

This was it, then. She'd seen how fast the Nazis executed people. There was no point in fighting. Kristina raised her empty hands above her head.

"Stand up," the soldier ordered.

It wasn't easy to stand in the cockpit. Kristina struggled to balance her feet between the rudder pedals in the tight space below the pilot's seat. She felt the soldier move the barrel of the gun away from her head and reposition it in the small of her back.

Kristina froze, her breath shaking now. A shot in the head would be fast and painless. But a shot in the lower back would mean a slow and agonising death. She didn't dare to move or even to speak.

"Are you ..." the voice behind her started, the tone rising oddly higher. It almost sounded as if it was a different speaker. Then the gruffness returned, and the soldier asked, "Are you armed?"

Kristina remembered the last time she'd held her pistol, when she'd been sheltering behind the oil drum.

"In my tunic pocket," she croaked. "The right pocket."

She felt the soldier fish around in her pocket and snag the pistol from her tunic.

Now she was completely defenceless.

"All right, get out," the soldier ordered. "Get out of the plane."

She felt the gun at her back fall away. Kristina sucked in a sobbing breath of relief, then braced herself with her hands against the sides of the cockpit. She got her feet up on the pilot's seat and turned to lower herself over the side of the plane.

It was then that she saw her attacker for the first time.

He stood in the rear cockpit pointing both guns at her.

He wasn't a Nazi soldier.

He was a child.

CHAPTER 10

The young boy wore a school tie and blazer.
He couldn't have been more than twelve years
old – if that. He had black hair and green eyes
that glinted like emeralds, and the whitest face
Kristina had ever seen. The knuckles of his
hands on the guns were also white with strain,
but the hands themselves were chapped raw and
red.

Those hands that held the heavy pistols didn't
shake. The boy was as steady as a rock. And the
look on his dirty face wasn't desperate, it was grim.

Kristina jumped from the plane and her feet hit
the ground. She stood back, still holding her hands
above her head to show her submission, and looked
up at her attacker. This boy might not have been
a Nazi soldier, but he was still aiming two pistols
at her from a metre away. Kristina thought he
wouldn't hesitate to shoot her as surely and swiftly
as an SS officer – if he decided he had to.

"What do you want?" Kristina asked.

"I want to get to England," the boy said.

If Kristina hadn't been so stunned with grief and fear, she'd have laughed.

"The best I can probably do is get you out of Poland," Kristina said. "I'm heading for Romania. But if you want to fly there in this plane, you'd better not shoot me."

The boy lowered the pistols, and Kristina lowered her arms.

She took a long, deep breath. The boy wasn't shaking, but Kristina was. She didn't want him to notice, and she dared to put her hands in the pockets of her tunic to hide them.

"Who are you?" Kristina asked.

"My name's Julian Srebro."

His voice was clear and youthful now. He'd been putting on the gruffness on purpose to fool her so he could disarm her. He was short and slender and small boned, and looked so light that Kristina thought she could sit on him in a fight – if he wasn't armed with two loaded guns.

"How did you get in my plane?" Kristina asked.

Julian frowned at her, as if she were asking a stupid question. "Climbed in last night while it was dark," he said. "And I couldn't get out this morning because of the battle."

"I mean, where did you come from?" Kristina said.

Julian spoke through his teeth, his voice now choking with rage and grief. "My father is – *was* – the headmaster at the Birky Language School and my mother was ... was Head of English. When the Germans came through the village yesterday, they just chucked everybody out of the school – like rat-catchers clearing a barn. They kicked the younger students out into the street and then took the fifth and sixth forms and the staff out on the playing field and shot them."

He was bitter and matter-of-fact as he continued, "They shot *all of them*. All the senior students and all the teachers, the dinner ladies and the boiler man – everybody. The younger kids watched through the fence. And then the Germans piled the bodies into a flat-bed lorry, and they shot at the little kids who ran after them."

Kristina felt her eyes going wide with horror. She'd heard terrible things about what the Nazi invaders did to Polish civilians, but this was the most horrendous thing she'd heard yet.

"How did you get away?" Kristina asked softly.

"I was hiding in my dad's office in the main building while it was going on," Julian said. "Dad saw the smoke, and the trucks coming up the drive, and sent me with his keys to get things out of his desk – the gun and … and other things. He told me to get out if he didn't come back, and to go to England. We've got family there. Dad told me I should run to the airstrip – the school wall ends just by the field there. He thought the airmen might help me."

Julian's eyes narrowed as he looked down at Kristina from the rear cockpit of the RWD-8. "Airwomen," he added. "Whatever. My dad was a pilot too – in the last war. There weren't any women flying back then. But you seem to know what you're doing."

"How old are you?" Kristina asked.

Julian murmured something that she couldn't hear. Whatever he'd said – fourteen, maybe, or fifteen – she could tell that he was lying.

Then he startled her by saying defiantly and loudly, "I'm eleven."

Julian had changed his mind and told her the truth.

"You were there while the battle was going on," Kristina said. "Did you see our P-11 fighter ram the Luftwaffe Messerschmitt?"

"Yes," Julian said. "I was already hiding in this plane by then, but I could look up and see what was going on in the sky."

"So you didn't see what happened after that?"

Kristina waited for Julian to answer, but he didn't say anything, so she told him.

"The Germans executed our pilot just after he landed."

"What did you expect them to do?" Julian asked.

"The pilot was my twin brother," Kristina told him. "Leopold Tomiak."

Julian was silent for a moment. Then he nodded slowly. "So you understand me," he said. "You're alone now too."

Kristina swallowed. She turned away and tried to think.

She couldn't leave this boy by himself here in the middle of nowhere.

Kristina had expected to go to Romania with Leopold to rejoin the Polish Air Force in exile. She still meant to stick to that plan, and it didn't include taking an eleven-year-old orphaned refugee. But she'd have to help Julian get out of Poland, to Romania, where he'd be safe from the invading German Army. Then she'd have to get rid of him.

"Give me back my gun," Kristina said.

Julian gazed down at her from his place in the rear cockpit. "All right," he said in a low voice.

Julian climbed out of the plane. It wasn't easy – in addition to the two guns, Julian had a school satchel that got in his way. Kristina held her breath, afraid he'd shoot her – or even himself – by accident. But Julian made it safely to the ground and gave Kristina back her pistol. She took it, put it away and held out her empty hand.

The boy hesitated. Then he reached out and shook Kristina's offered hand carefully. His fingers felt cold and small. Touching his skin made Kristina realise with a jolt how young – and how alone – he really was.

There was no sound but birdsong and the rustling of the leaves of the apple trees overhead in the wind.

"I guess we're going to have apples for dinner," Kristina said. "I'm going to need more fuel to get to Romania, and I don't want to waste the afternoon hunting for it only to get stuck at another airfield that's under siege. I can't fly at night, so we'll wait till tomorrow morning to look for fuel." She saw the flaw in her plan even as she spoke. "I guess that's a gamble too – maybe there won't be any place left that hasn't fallen to the Germans. But if I take off now, I'm worried I'll fall asleep in the air. So we'll have to spend the night here. It won't be very comfortable, but I think the best thing to do is to try to sleep in the plane—"

"Oh!" Julian interrupted. "You said 'we'?"

"I'm not going to leave you here," Kristina snapped.

Julian let out a heavy sigh of relief. "So I can come with you?" he said. "Thank you, Miss ... Miss Tomiak, right?"

Kristina wasn't going to be won over by his exaggerated politeness. "I'll take you out of Poland," she said. "Don't expect me to fly you to England. And it's Lieutenant Tomiak to you."

"You haven't got a pilot's badge," Julian pointed out.

Kristina answered him with her teeth clenched. "That's because my brother was wearing mine when they shot him."

Julian said nothing for a moment. Then, to her surprise, he gave her a salute, and said, "Thank you, Lieutenant Tomiak."

CHAPTER 11

Kristina slept badly. She was cramped and cold and uncomfortable in the pilot's cockpit of the RWD-8. She dozed and woke and dozed again to hideous dreams of Leopold and blood.

Julian wasn't awake by the time it was finally light enough for her to take off the next morning. He was sleeping like a brick in the seat behind Kristina. He was so much smaller than she was that he could curl like a kitten behind the control column. Kristina was envious of his small child's ability to sleep anywhere, a knack she'd lost at least five years ago.

She waited for Julian to wake up. She couldn't force herself to disturb him. But he slept on and on. Kristina grew nervous. She needed to get moving – she needed to know what was happening outside this orchard full of birdsong. She stuffed her pockets with apples for later and started up the plane without waking the boy.

After flying for a short time, Kristina came to a road. Below her, a steady stream of buses and cars and horse-drawn wagons were fleeing south, trying to get out of Poland as the German Army invaded. She realised how lucky she was to be in the air.

After she'd flown for another fifteen minutes, she came to the railway line that led to Lvov. Now she knew where she was – most of the way to Stanislavov. Still in Poland, but maybe the Germans hadn't reached this far south yet. Kristina gave a yell of excitement when she spotted the Stanislavov Flight School airfield and saw three RWD-8s just like hers parked on the grass below.

"YES!"

Finally one thing had gone smoothly. She needed fuel, and here was the peaceful Stanislavov airfield full of Polish planes and maybe fuel as well. Kristina glided down onto the grass. A few people gathered in front of the clubhouse to watch as she landed.

She didn't really want to have to explain Julian to them, so she parked her plane a good distance away from the building and the other planes. Kristina shut down the engine and turned around to see the boy sitting up in the rear cockpit. His green eyes glinted in his pale, smudged face.

"Keep your head down," Kristina told Julian. "I don't think I'm supposed to be carrying a stowaway. I have to go and see if I can find us some fuel, and I don't want a little kid tagging along behind me."

"Are we out of Poland yet?" Julian asked as he slid down so that his head was below the rim of the open cockpit. Now he couldn't be seen by anyone outside the plane.

"No," Kristina said. "We need to get fuel first. And they might not have any here."

"And they'll make you pay for it if they do, right?" Julian asked.

"Wow, I hope not!" Kristina said. She hadn't even the smallest copper change – there was nothing in her pockets but apples and her pistol. "They're supposed to be stockpiling supplies for the Air Force so that they can retreat."

"And *you're* the Air Force," Julian remarked.

He didn't add "what's left of it". But Kristina knew Julian was thinking it. His desperate attempt at humour reminded her painfully of Leopold.

"I'm the Air Force," Kristina agreed.

She reached back and handed Julian a couple of apples from the orchard. The morning was half gone, and she guessed he was hungry.

"Present from the Air Force," she said. "A bit late. At least they're sweet."

To her surprise, Julian's face lit up. He gave her a wonderful beaming half smile, as if she'd done something really thoughtful.

"Just a sec – don't go yet ..." Julian said, and stuffed the apples in the pockets of his blazer. He rooted around in his school satchel for a minute, then held out one red chapped hand in a closed fist and pressed something into Kristina's palm.

"Present from the Birky Language School," Julian said.

She opened her hand. He'd given her two chocolate coins wrapped in gold foil.

"Chocolate and apples!" Kristina said. "Best breakfast you'll get till the war is over." She put the coins in her pocket. "I'm going to find out if I can get fuel. You stay here."

She climbed out of the RWD-8 and warned Julian, "Don't let anyone see you."

CHAPTER 12

There weren't many people about. Kristina couldn't tell if that was because the retreating Polish Air Force hadn't arrived yet or because they'd already left. The men who'd come out to watch her land looked grim and tired but also curious. There were three tanker lorries parked behind the three RWD-8s.

Kristina approached the small group of mechanics. They studied her, recognised her uniform, and one of them put out a grubby hand for her to shake. His unshaven young face peered out from under the shadow of his cap's visor.

"Hey there!" Kristina said. "What's the news?"

"Welcome!" the mechanic said. "Everyone else seems to have been shot down, and these flight-school planes of ours aren't of any use – they can't fly far. We're just about to drive these lorries over the border and out of Poland ourselves, to stop the fuel being snatched up by the enemy when they get here."

"You've got fuel, then?" Kristina said, hugely relieved.

"Not to waste on your dinky RWD-8, we don't," the mechanic said. "If you'd brought us a P-11 fighter, it would be another story. You can come with us in the lorries if you want."

"Are you meeting up with an Air Force unit in Romania?" Kristina asked.

The mechanic rolled his eyes. "Where have you been?" he asked. "Nobody's meeting up in Romania. That was yesterday. Ah well, we probably have the last working radio set in Poland, so not everybody's heard the news. This morning the Russians joined forces with Germany and invaded us from the east. They'll probably get here later today. All our defences have collapsed. We're finished."

It seemed like the end of the world.

Kristina was so stunned she couldn't speak. The young mechanic added, as if trying to give her a grain of good news, "Anyone who can get to France is supposed to regroup there."

"*France!*" Kristina gasped, finding her voice again. It was the other side of Europe, thousands of kilometres away. "What about Romania? How is everyone supposed to get to *France?*"

"Slowly, I guess," the mechanic said. "If we can get across Hungary, the Polish embassy in Budapest is issuing new passports to help us get to France. And the Romanian and Hungarian authorities are organising refugee camps for Polish evacuees where we can wait."

Kristina guessed what those foreign refugee camps would be like: disorganised, lots of forms, terrible food. Worse than being part of the retreating army. The chances were low of getting quickly to the Polish embassy in the Hungarian capital city of Budapest, especially without her own plane.

The mechanic had offered to drive her over the Polish border. Would he be willing to take Julian along too?

Would Julian even want to go? Kristina didn't think she could convince him that a refugee camp would help get him to his family in England.

She needed to keep her plane. She needed fuel.

"I'm not flying a fighter plane, but I'm a liaison pilot," Kristina said. "If you give me all the information your radio operator learned this morning, I can take it straight to Budapest today, ahead of the ground troops. My plane has an extra fuel tank and can fly twice as far as your flight-school aircraft. Come and refuel it, and you can have this …"

She reached into her pocket and tossed one of Julian's gold chocolate coins in the air. It spun, twinkling dully in the morning light. Kristina snatched it out of the air as it came back down. Then she ran back towards her plane.

The young mechanic jumped into one of the lorries and followed her.

Kristina realised too late that the mechanic would be able to see inside the rear cockpit when he climbed up to the wing to fill the extra tank with fuel. He'd see Julian hiding.

But she had a head start on the lorry. When she reached her plane, Kristina pulled off her Air Force tunic and threw it over the rear cockpit. She prayed that Julian had the sense to sit still and keep his head down. Then she rolled up her sleeves as if she meant business and climbed up on top of the plane to open the fuel cap.

When the lorry pulled up, Kristina hopped down and strode forwards boldly to unhook the petrol hose. The young mechanic got out a ladder so he could climb up to the wing tank, and Kristina handed the pump up to him. He didn't say anything. He clearly wanted to get the job over with as fast as she did, before anybody questioned him about putting fuel into a mere RWD-8.

When he'd finished, the mechanic held out a dirty palm, waiting for Kristina's promised payment.

Kristina dropped Julian's two chocolate coins into his hand.

The young man stared at the sweets for a moment. Kristina held her breath. She had nothing else to pay him with. She hadn't *said* she'd give him anything other than the foil disc she'd flashed in the air. He might report her to someone …

In desperation, Kristina offered the mechanic an apple as well. "They're good and sweet," she said.

To her surprise, the young man burst out laughing. Joy – real joy – changed his face. It was the exact look she'd seen for a moment on Julian's face earlier.

"All right," the mechanic said. "Good and sweet wishes to you too." He pocketed the coins and took the apple.

Kristina was baffled.

"Now get the hell out of here," the mechanic added. "Good luck getting to Budapest." He jumped back into his lorry without another word and drove off.

CHAPTER 13

Kristina climbed back into the pilot's cockpit of her RWD-8. She leaned back and asked Julian, "Did you see what happened there?"

The boy was still hidden beneath Kristina's tunic in the seat behind her. His answer was muffled, but Kristina was amazed to hear laughter in his voice as well.

"The driver thought you were Jewish," Julian hissed with delight. "You gave him an apple and something sweet to go with it. He thought you were wishing him a sweet new year. It was Rosh Hashanah three days ago, the Jewish new year. You're supposed to give people apples and honey when you wish them a sweet new year, but I guess that when you're waiting for an invading army to turn up, chocolate works too."

Suddenly Kristina saw Julian in a new light.

"Are *you* Jewish?" she asked.

"I thought you knew that!" he replied. "Why do you think I want to go to England? You think Hitler's going to be nicer to Polish Jews than he is to German Jews? You think the Nazis aren't going to burn our temples and smash up our shops here just like they did back in Germany? And he's not going to stop at Poland either. Dad was in the last war and he says – *said* – it's just a matter of time before the trenches open up in France and Belgium again. Only now the bombs and guns will be bigger."

There had been Jewish people all over Warsaw, but Kristina hadn't known much about them. They'd mostly gone to their own schools, spoken their own language, shopped for their own food in their own shops. An image came to her mind of an old bearded man she'd seen once, wearing a hat and a prayer shawl embroidered with unreadable script. He'd rocked gently as he'd read from a book on a park bench. He'd seemed so mysterious, so *different*, that Kristina had been a bit frightened.

This small, fierce boy in her plane was mysterious and different too. And also, perhaps, a bit frightening.

But it wasn't because Julian was Jewish, Kristina realised. It was because he was *Julian*: clever and ruthless and full of surprises.

"We should have gone to England last year," Julian said bitterly. "My father left it too late. He didn't want to let down the school. But he knew what was coming – I mean, we all knew, didn't we? Sort of."

"We didn't know it would be as bad as it is," Kristina said. She looked up at the sky as she leaned back to talk to him. "We didn't know the Russians would join the Germans. That's what just happened this morning. And even up until yesterday, we thought we'd be able to do something to stop the worst from happening. You don't believe the worst is going to happen until it's actually here."

Yesterday. It had only been *yesterday*, and the day before, for both of them.

Kristina saw again Leopold's blood spattering across the windscreen of his P-11 and squeezed her eyes shut.

After a moment, she drew in a sharp breath and opened her eyes. She couldn't afford to waste time sitting here. It wouldn't be long before German soldiers arrived – or Russian ones.

"The plan's changed again since the Russians have invaded us too," Kristina said. "I'm supposed to join the Polish Air Force in France now. But I don't think I'll be able to fly all the way there, and I have to go to Budapest to get a passport first. You can come with me and get a passport too."

"I have a passport," Julian told her. "Well, I have Dad's passport, and it's got my name on it. I found it in his desk with his other things. And the chocolate coins. We have family in New York as well as London, and the New York ones always send us chocolate coins for Hanukkah. But that's months away. Dad must have been saving the coins, hiding them until later, because they were with the gun and the money and the maps—"

Kristina jerked her head around, interrupting Julian, "You have—"

"Not *much* money," he said hastily.

But it wasn't money she wanted.

"*Maps!* You have maps?" Kristina cried. "Stop talking and hand them over."

She reached one expectant hand back towards the rear cockpit. She heard Julian shuffling around behind her, and then she closed her fingers over a thick wad of folded linen paper. He'd just handed her the one thing that might prove to be just as precious as fuel.

She laid the maps in her lap and steadied her trembling hands against the RWD-8's control column. Then Kristina flicked through the small collection.

There was a tattered school map of Poland, showing different geographical areas. There was a new map swallowing up Austria, Czechoslovakia and Germany as "Greater Germany" – well, that was only helpful if you wanted to avoid it. A road atlas for Northern Italy was more useful, but she'd have to get there first.

And then Kristina struck gold – a tourist map of the Carpathian Mountains. She would have to cross them if she wanted to fly straight to Budapest.

Julian waited behind her, still hidden beneath Kristina's tunic, full of secret grief and determination. She wanted to get rid of him as soon as she possibly could, but there was no doubt that it was useful having him along with her. There was the pistol that he wasn't afraid to use, the magical chocolate coins that had fuelled her plane, and now these maps. What else was Julian hiding in his schoolbag of tricks?

"Julian, do you have a notebook and pencil?" Kristina asked.

"Here," he replied.

She reached back into the cockpit and found his small, cold, rough hand offering her exactly what she'd asked for.

"Can you keep watch for me?" Kristina said. "Peek out on each side and let me know if you see anyone coming to check us out." Kristina felt nervous now about keeping her head down in the cockpit. She didn't want to be taken by surprise by anyone, friend or foe. "I need a bit of time to plan a route."

"All right," Julian said.

Next stop, Budapest, Kristina thought. *Just as soon as we conquer the Carpathians.*

CHAPTER 14

It was over five hundred kilometres to Budapest, and Kristina reckoned she had plenty of fuel with her tanks full. It would take about five hours. But from looking at the map, the navigation wouldn't be as difficult as she'd feared. She could follow the railroad, and that would guide her over the Carpathian Mountains. After that, she would pick up the Tisa River for the second part of the journey.

Kristina folded the map carefully, so she'd be able to refer to it in flight. Then she climbed out of the plane once more. No one was nearby.

"Jump out quick," she told Julian. "Have a pee behind the wing if you need to and then get back in. I'll go around the other side – it'll be faster than taking turns."

Julian was fast and careful while climbing out and was back in the rear cockpit before Kristina had put her tunic on again and was ready to swing the propeller.

Kristina couldn't see another plane anywhere in the sky as she took off. But to the north and the east, ominous trails of black smoke rose here and there, darkening the horizons. Poland was burning.

Kristina flew south-west.

*

The calm of the cold sky above the Carpathian peaks felt dreamlike after yesterday's hellish horror. Shreds of mountain cloud tore over the forests and valleys below. The green tips of trees were now beginning to fade to autumn colours of gold and tawny brown.

Kristina flew high. It was cold at two thousand metres above sea level, but she would use less fuel flying high, and it was safer to be well above the mountain tops. She didn't dare go much higher for fear of not being able to breathe. Kristina and Julian didn't have flight helmets, and they couldn't talk to each other in the air.

Somewhere down below, the Polish Army was retreating. Civilians were fleeing, ripe grain was burning, people were arguing over train fares and passports, children were crying, wounded soldiers were bleeding. Up here there was nothing but wind and the beautiful mountain landscape rolling away endlessly on all sides.

Kristina could see the fine thread of the railroad as it wound its way across the landscape, but she couldn't see any boundaries anywhere. The world was all one enormous tapestry.

Her tears dried cold on her face in the high wind.

*

After two hours freezing her face off flying into a headwind, Kristina came to the spot between two small towns where the railway line crossed the Tisa River.

She changed her course to follow the Tisa – even though the sky was empty, she felt safer away from the railroad.

A few minutes later, Kristina landed in a field so she and Julian could stretch their legs. They ate the last of the apples but saved Julian's stash of chocolate coins. Kristina thought she'd never been so hungry in her life.

"Everything looks so *peaceful* from high up," Julian said.

"I know," Kristina said. She watched the boy scratching at the skin of his knuckles and saw the backs of his fists were raw. "What's wrong with your hands?" she asked.

"Eczema," Julian replied. "It gets worse when I'm upset. My hands were fine last week. Now I just want to tear them off. Is it much further to Budapest?"

"Another two or three hours," Kristina told him. "But I won't have to fly so high, so it won't be as cold."

"When we get there, I can help you get your passport at the embassy," Julian said.

Kristina thought this was highly unlikely. "Do you speak Hungarian?" she asked.

"Better than that. I speak *German*. My parents ran a language school," Julian reminded her. "I speak French too. You could take me to France with you – it would get me closer to England."

"I expect someone in authority will take the plane away from me once we get to Budapest," Kristina said. "It'll be assigned to someone more important. Polish planes are worth their weight in gold now, even unarmed ones like mine. Most of our combat aircraft have been shot down. We'll have to fly French planes when we regroup. So once we've sorted out the passports, you're on your own."

Julian's expression turned bleak and distant, and his green eyes were unreadable.

"There are trains and you have money," Kristina told him heartlessly. "Just make sure you stay out of Greater Germany."

*

The Tisa River wound southward within a wide green plain. Kristina knew that she would easily find her way to Budapest by picking up the railroad again at a river crossing about a hundred kilometres south of the city. Then all she had to do was follow the train tracks until she reached Budapest.

But as she flew on that clear September afternoon, something new began to make her uneasy.

Kristina wasn't flying as high now, and she could see more detail on the ground below. Wherever there was a railroad junction or a train station, crowds of people were waiting. A river of trucks and buses seemed to move slowly to and from these meeting places, collecting and distributing people. She saw large canvas tents being erected in town squares, and people waiting outside schools and civic buildings.

It didn't take much imagination to guess what was going on: the Hungarian authorities were trying to set up a system to deal with the thousands of Polish refugees who had fled to the safety of their nearest neighbours.

Kristina didn't believe she'd get to jump to the front of any of those queues just because she was an Air Force liaison pilot. And she knew that Julian would be right at the back – a half-grown Jewish boy all by himself.

It will be better when you get closer to Budapest, Leopold's voice in her head told her cheerfully, as Kristina sat alone in the windy pilot's cockpit with her thoughts.

But it wasn't better. The railway junctions were bigger here. In one place she flew over what looked like an entire temporary town in a school playing field. It had been filled with tents and makeshift sheds.

Julian saw it too. Kristina turned around to look at him, and he was half standing in his cockpit, gripping the sides of the seat as he looked down. His black hair whipped in the wind and his teeth were bared and clenched. Julian looked as if he were in pain.

He was too clever not to know that this would be his future.

Maybe if I go to the far side of the city, the routes in will be less crowded, Kristina thought.

She didn't see an airfield and she didn't even know if one existed. She couldn't take the plane right into the centre of Budapest. She had less than an hour's flying time of fuel left.

She was going to have to land.

CHAPTER 15

Kristina flew low over an area of rich, sprawling houses on the western outskirts of the city. In the golden sunlight of the early September evening she found the perfect landing place: an empty football field at the edge of a park.

She touched down lightly on the grass. Between the football field and a nearby tram stop was a grove of pine trees with an open-air picnic pavilion beneath them. The ordinary, pretty scene seemed more than five hundred kilometres away from yesterday's battle at Birky. It was so peaceful that it was confusing.

Kristina shut down the engine.

"Well, here we are," she announced. "We'll have to walk or see if someone can give us a ride into the city."

"We can take the tram," Julian said behind her. "But won't the embassy be closed? It's Sunday."

Kristina leaned her head against the plane's control column, suddenly exhausted. Where were they going to sleep? Wouldn't there be an enormous queue at the passport office, even if it wasn't open? Should they get in line and spend the night there, holding their places? What about food? She was starving. Five hours of flying in one day was hard work, even in peacetime. Kristina had never been in the air for so long with nothing in her stomach but a few apples, or on so little sleep.

Julian was hungry too, but not as tired. He was still thinking clearly.

"There's a garage over there by the tram stop, and a petrol station," he said. "Let's see if we can get something to eat there."

"You said you have money – is it Hungarian money?" Kristina asked.

"Some of it. And some in other currencies too," Julian answered. "It was part of Dad's plan for getting to England."

Kristina noticed that he didn't tell her how much money he had.

"You could refuel your plane," Julian said.

Kristina hadn't even thought about refuelling the plane. She'd been focused on handing it back to the Air Force once she found someone with the proper authority. But of course a pilot would have to fly the plane out of this football field. Maybe Kristina herself would have to come back for it. And it would be much more useful full of fuel than empty.

"These people aren't going to be like the mechanics back in Poland," Kristina said. "They'll make us pay, and I don't have any money ..."

"Kristina, I'll pay," Julian said, climbing out of the rear cockpit. "I'll pay, and then we can go to France together."

And there it was again: Leopold's voice in her head.

Wouldn't it be amazing to fly to France all the way from Poland? Leopold said.

It was almost as if he were speaking to her. She could imagine *so clearly* exactly what Leopold would say, what he'd do.

Think of it – soaring over the beautiful French Riviera coast! his voice came again. *You have your own plane. What do you want to stand in line at the embassy for?*

Kristina raised her head from the control column. She turned to look over at the petrol station. Petrol used for cars wouldn't be as efficient in the RWD-8 as aircraft fuel, but the sturdy little plane could run on it without damaging the engine.

A green car drove slowly past but didn't stop. Nobody else was around. The scene seemed utterly untouched by the onset of war. But Kristina had seen the crowds, the queues, the tents – she knew what was coming.

Get some petrol and fly to France! Leopold's voice told her.

"You need to get fuel while they still have some," Julian said wisely.

Kristina climbed out of the plane. She faced Julian with her hands on her hips. The boy stood looking up at her, his green eyes sunken in his tired, pinched face. He was haunted by the deaths of his parents just the way Kristina was haunted by the death of her brother.

Julian spoke German and French. He had money – he could pay for fuel. He had maps – Kristina couldn't navigate without them. He had a passport.

Kristina had nothing. She didn't even have her silver Air Force pilot's badge, the fierce white eagle of Poland.

All that she had was her plane.

If she kept flying – if they went *over* the queues and the camps, the checkpoints and the roadblocks – maybe they could avoid any registration until they got to France. After all, there was a Polish embassy in Paris too.

"All right," Kristina said to Julian. "I bet they've never fuelled up a plane here before."

Then, knowing what Leopold would have said, she added, "It'll be fun."

PART 3: *Exile*

CHAPTER 16

The petrol station looked closed, but it had a small ice-cream kiosk attached to it, which was open. It was run by a young couple, and the woman was able to understand a little German. Julian spun a story to them about how he was flying from Austria to Italy as a challenge for the Scouts. He told them he'd come via Budapest to avoid crossing the Alps, and that Kristina was a famous Russian (*Russian!*) aviator who'd been hired as his instructor.

Julian got away with it somehow. He made this unlikely story seem possible. He was an appealing small boy, so earnest and determined, with his neat blazer and tie and leather school satchel. Plus he really had arrived in an aeroplane that needed refuelling. The young man agreed to open up the garage for them.

When he'd paid for the fuel, Julian whipped out a notebook and got the man to sign and date it. Julian carefully logged the time and place next to his signature.

All Kristina had to do was keep her mouth shut and show the couple how to fill the tanks. They couldn't get the plane right up to the pumps, so it had to be done by hand, and they made ten trips back and forth in total with a twenty-litre fuel can and a funnel. But Julian's fake story and real enthusiasm caught the couple's attention and they both helped to get the job done.

Julian also managed to buy two car blankets (woven with the crest of the local football team) as well as a bag of fried dough piled with cheese, a winter salami and two bottles of milk. And he somehow arranged for the toilet in the back of the petrol station to be left open for them all night if they wanted it. The young woman gave them free ice cream.

Afterwards, Kristina and Julian sat at one of the picnic tables in the pavilion with their maps spread. They worked out the next leg of their journey in full view of everyone who came and went from the small park.

Every now and then someone would approach them and ask curious questions about the plane. One old man walking a huge deerhound paced around the RWD-8 knowingly. He had a curious expression on his face and was shaking his head.

Then he spent a long time chatting to Julian in German.

Kristina saw Julian growing more and more nervous as they spoke. His pale face became white and his eyes narrowed to green slits. His replies to the old man got shorter and simpler. Kristina couldn't understand the conversation, but she could tell that the man was mining Julian for details that he didn't know.

At last the old man turned to Kristina and shook hands with her cheerfully. Then he whistled to his dog and turned to go. He stumped away, muttering a name Kristina had never heard before: "Olga Shostakovich! Olga Shostakovich!"

"Why did you have to tell everybody I'm *Russian*?" Kristina asked Julian, when the man was too far away to hear. "The Russians are the invaders – our enemies! Allied with the Germans! I don't want to pretend to be Russian!"

"And I don't want to pretend to be *Austrian*," Julian snapped. "They're already part of Greater Germany. But if I say you're all that's left of the Polish Air Force and I'm a Jewish refugee, where's that going to get us?"

Julian rubbed the backs of his itchy hands against the buckles of his schoolbag.

"Don't scratch," Kristina told him. "What did that man with the dog say to you? And who's Olga ... Olga what's-her-name?"

"He wanted to know what your name was," Julian replied. "So I had to make it up fast, something that sounded really Russian. The only surnames I could think of fast were all composers – that's how I came up with Olga Shostakovich. He seemed impressed!" Some colour was coming back into Julian's face now that the encounter with the man was over. "And he told us not to fly near the Polish border because Germany and Poland are at war."

"Oh, thanks, mister," Kristina said.

"He knew our plane was Polish because of the checkerboard flag on the side. I said my dad had won it in a card game. The man also said the Nazis banned the Scouts in Austria last year, and I think he might be right." Julian rubbed his eyes with his red, chapped knuckles. "I thought my story was going to fall apart, so I said I was part of an international unit called the Young Explorers. The man had never heard of that, of course, because

I'd made it up. I don't know if anything like that exists."

Julian lowered his hands, blinking. He took a deep, ragged breath and finished, "I told him we're going to Italy tomorrow. That's right, isn't it?"

"I hope so," Kristina said. Flying was exhausting, but dealing with suspicious strangers in an unfamiliar language was just as difficult in its own way. "From here, Trieste is about as far as we went today, and we have more mountains to cross. I wish ..."

"You wish you had a decent bed to sleep in?" Julian asked.

Kristina thought of the alternatives to spending the night on a park bench under a car blanket. They could be in a military field tent full of people fleeing their homes, or on the pavement outside the Polish embassy in Budapest.

"I wish you'd teach me a little bit of French," she said.

Julian gave her one of his rare real smiles. "I would love to."

CHAPTER 17

For a few hours, Kristina slept without dreaming.

Then in the middle of the night, she was woken by the wind. It tossed the branches of the surrounding trees and shook pine cones down to drum on the cast-iron roof of the pavilion. The sound of the wind was soothing, like the ocean's surf crashing on a beach. Kristina lay awake, rolled up in her souvenir blanket, and listened to the rustling of pine needles.

Then she heard something else: quiet, muffled sobs that came from the bench that stood back to back against hers.

Listening to Julian's private grief reminded Kristina of her own. Tears began to run down her face. And it was too much to bear alone.

Kristina reached between the slats of the bench, found Julian's thin, cold hand and grasped his fingers.

After a while, the tears dried on her face, and she drifted off to sleep again. But she didn't let go of Julian's hand.

*

Kristina woke at first light with a feeling of dread in her stomach.

A thousand kilometres lay between Budapest and the French border, and it was another thousand to Paris. But it was the first thousand that worried Kristina. At least two full days of flight lay ahead of her, and negotiating for fuel and food in languages she didn't speak. She was worried about crossing the high ground and steep valleys of the Karst Plateau in the Kingdom of Yugoslavia. Most of all, she was afraid of travelling across Italy, a Fascist country allied with Germany.

But Italy aren't fighting with them, Leopold's ever-cheerful voice in her head reminded her.

"Not yet," Kristina said aloud to herself. She and Julian would just have to keep up the dramatic act of being Russian and Austrian, and hope nobody questioned the proud checkerboard Polish Air Force flag painted on the plane.

Kristina knew they wouldn't be able to stop at a real airfield until she got to France. She wasn't going to be able to get a qualified mechanic to check the plane or even to fuel it. She was going to have to land in meadows and car parks, to organise petrol at car garages like a tourist on a holiday. Otherwise people would sooner or later ask her to produce official documents that she didn't have.

While Julian still slept, curled like a kitten again on his park bench, Kristina gave her plane as much attention as she could. She checked the control lines and all the moving surfaces of the wings and tail. Everything seemed fine. There wasn't any reason it *shouldn't* be fine. The plane was often in the air five hours every day.

The sun rose in a mass of rosy pink clouds – a beautiful start to another beautiful September day. The weather had been so good during Germany's invasion of Poland that Kristina had begun to hate the sun. A cloudy sky over Warsaw might have stopped the Luftwaffe from bombing it so easily; rain might have slowed down the German Army.

But the fluffy pink clouds piling up in the west were making Kristina uneasy. Rain, now? She didn't want to have to fly into bad weather.

She woke Julian. They each ate half a stale dough cake, trying to save some for later, but the boy wouldn't touch the salami.

"There's still plenty," Kristina said. "Go ahead and have some."

"I got it for you," Julian answered. "You're the one doing all the hard work. And I don't like salami anyway."

Kristina and Julian took off in the plane before the garage opened up, meaning they couldn't get any more food.

You know, the kid probably doesn't eat pork, Leopold's voice told Kristina. *He's Jewish.*

Of course Julian didn't eat pork.

But he hadn't made a fuss about it. He'd just gone hungry.

I wonder what else he's hiding from you, Kristina's brother teased in her head.

*

Kristina flew south of Lake Balaton. It was a good navigation marker – a long body of water that was easy to spot from far away. There were more of the refugee camps here as well. Kristina didn't want to land anywhere near them.

She broke the journey near a small farm in Yugoslavia, to rest and eat a bit more before she tackled the dramatic hills and valleys of the Karst Plateau. The sky was now grey and overcast, and Kristina didn't trust it.

She was right to be worried. After another hour's flight, the little RWD-8 was surrounded by storm clouds.

The wind increased without Kristina being aware of it at first. Then it worsened and the little plane was buffeted, lifted and tossed about like a scrap of newspaper. Kristina couldn't fly in the straight line she'd planned – she had to avoid the black clouds that kept rising ahead of her, hiding the horizon.

Kristina didn't have the flight instruments or the training to fly without being able to see the ground. She would rather face a Luftwaffe Messerschmitt than fly into a black cloud twice as high as the Carpathian Mountains, sizzling with flashes of lightning.

The RWD-8 swooped and bucked. Behind her, Julian grabbed Kristina's shoulder. She shook him off – she needed her full concentration to control the plane.

Big ice-cold raindrops stung her cheeks as she flew. She glanced back at Julian and saw that he was being sick over the side of the rear cockpit.

Kristina felt sick too – not just with the way the plane rocked in the wind but also with fear. Trying to fly through a storm like this could only end in disaster. But there was no place to land: below her she saw nothing but rocky slopes and dark trees bending in the wind. The bottom of the clouds kept forcing her to fly lower and lower, driving the plane towards the treetops. She was sandwiched between blinding clouds and unforgiving forest and rock.

Kristina didn't even know which country she was flying over. It might still be Yugoslavia; it might be Italy. She didn't care any more: she just wanted to be safely on the ground.

Then, suddenly, the ground dropped away below her.

It happened so quickly it was confusing. One moment the trees were rising to meet the wheels of the RWD-8, and the next moment Kristina was sailing five hundred metres above a great green plain.

She'd made it over the Karst Plateau. She'd made it to the Italian border.

The clouds ahead were too thick and too low for Kristina to be able to see the Adriatic Sea ahead of her. There was no sign of the city of Trieste either. But she didn't want to land close to the city anyway. She descended fast, looking for somewhere like the friendly park they'd left back in Budapest that morning, before the storm.

CHAPTER 18

Kristina landed in the middle of a crossroads, close to a petrol station and small tourist campsite. Everything was shuttered against the rain. She parked at the edge of the turning circle for the petrol pumps, off the road, with the plane facing into the wind. She found a couple of rocks to wedge the wheels with. She wished she could tie down the wings, but she didn't have any rope.

While she was working, Julian managed to crawl out of the rear cockpit. He was sick again the moment his feet hit the ground. After that, he sat huddled against the plane, trying to stay out of the rain and waiting for Kristina.

Kristina didn't feel sick any more, but her head ached with hunger and strain and exhaustion.

"Do you have any aspirin in your magic bag of tricks?" she asked Julian.

Just then, a burly man with the good looks of a film star came running out of a small wooden office building. He shielded his head from the rain with a newspaper and joined Kristina beneath the wing of the RWD-8. He shook her hand and kissed her on both cheeks, welcoming Kristina with astonishment, and asked her a torrent of questions that she couldn't understand.

"Olga ... Olga Shostakovich," Kristina said hesitantly.

"Ah!" the man exclaimed, as if he understood now who she was. He looked her up and down, smiled, and then gave her a wink and a gentle pinch at her waistline.

Kristina took a step away from him, feeling awkward and embarrassed.

Julian emerged from under the other wing, looking very pale indeed. He straightened his tie and reached into his schoolbag for his notebook.

Julian *didn't* magically turn out to speak Italian. And the handsome man didn't seem to speak any German or French or Polish. The entire transaction for fuel was accomplished by Julian drawing pictures in his notebook and the man marking prices next to them.

But in the end, in addition to refilling the plane with fuel, the man insisted on giving them one of the pretty little tourist cabins to stay in that night, along with bread and cheese and a jug of milk. The cabin was one tiny room made of rustic wood, which just about fitted a double bed and a dresser with a washbasin on it next to the single window. The bed was covered with a yellow gingham bedspread and the basin was full of clean water. Julian opened the shutters and leaned out – the rain had stopped.

"I don't like that man," Julian said darkly as he turned back to Kristina. "The fuel cost a lot more than it did yesterday, and I think he overcharged us. But he threw in the food and bed, so I didn't argue."

Kristina hadn't liked the man either, with his winks and pinches. She was annoyed that she hadn't been able to join in the negotiation. "Maybe you got the charges mixed up," she suggested.

"It's very clear on the receipt," Julian insisted.

"Let me see."

Julian showed Kristina, but she struggled to read the man's writing. Her head was pounding. "You negotiate everything before I can ask you about it or check the figures," Kristina complained.

Julian didn't defend himself. He dodged out of the tiny room. "I'll let you wash up first," he said bluntly. "Take as long as you like." Then he slammed the solid wooden door behind him.

For a moment Kristina hesitated, nearly going after him. She still hoped he might have some aspirin in his satchel.

The boy's right, you know, Leopold said to Kristina in her head. *You would feel better after a bath. Still, if you want to go on being grubby as well as hungry and tired and scared ...*

It was a silly argument to have with herself. There wasn't any possibility of a real bath. But Kristina could wash up at the old-fashioned china basin, with a matching china saucer on the washstand holding a sliver of orange-blossom soap.

Kristina took off her tunic and blouse to strip to her underwear. She used a corner of the towel to scrub her arms and neck and face. The cool water was a blessing on her aching head.

She was in the middle of doing this, with her eyes squeezed shut and her face covered with soapsuds, when the handsome man came in quietly, without knocking.

Kristina heard the man bolt the door behind him as she frantically tried to rinse the soap from her face without getting it in her eyes.

CHAPTER 19

Kristina straightened up, her face and fringe dripping wet. A corner of the bed was between her and the man.

His expression was friendly, almost foolish, not a bit threatening – but Kristina was half naked and he'd locked the door, and she felt threatened anyway. She snatched up her blouse.

Shaking his head, the man quickly stepped around the bed towards Kristina, still wearing that foolish, friendly smile. He twitched the blouse from her hands, touching it gingerly as if he was offended at how dirty it was. To Kristina's shock he tossed the blouse under the bed.

Then the man turned back to her and gently caressed her bare arm.

An image of Leopold flashed across Kristina's vision. He was full of outraged fury as he leaped to her defence.

But there was no Leopold. Kristina was on her own.

There's a gun in your tunic pocket.

Kristina inched sideways, trying to reach her tunic where she'd dropped it on the yellow bedspread. The man put his other hand around her bare waist, trapping her. He bent his face towards hers for a kiss, and without thinking Kristina gave his cheek a resounding slap.

The man grabbed her wrists in self-defence, and he was stronger than Kristina. Now, even if he hadn't meant to frighten her, it was turning into a fight.

Kristina found herself every bit as frightened as she'd been when the German soldier had trapped her at the end of his rifle. She couldn't wrench her wrists free of the man's grip, so she kicked at her attacker's shins.

The bolted door rattled.

"Julian!" Kristina cried out. "The window!"

The man turned to check the door with a glance, then swung back to Kristina. He winked again and shrugged. He was clearly telling her that the boy wasn't going to be able to interrupt them.

But Julian didn't waste any time. Within thirty seconds, he was climbing in the open window. He hauled his small, thin body up over the window frame like a frantic wildcat, got himself in and sat on the sill, panting. Julian held his father's pistol in both his chafed hands, pointing it steady at the man's face.

"Get out!" Julian yelled.

The man burst out laughing and took a swipe at Julian, grabbing for the gun.

Julian sprang from the windowsill to the bed, vaulting over Kristina's head. She ducked to avoid his legs and backed against the bed. Julian crouched behind Kristina, leaning over her shoulder, still aiming the pistol at the threatening man.

The man did nothing but stand there shaking his head and smiling, so Julian fired a shot past him. The bullet shattered the china washbasin.

Julian stood on the bed, brandishing his pistol, and the man backed away. Now his expression was a mixture of fright and anger.

The man mimed sweeping with a dustpan and brush. Then he unbolted the door and stormed out.

Julian didn't put the gun away.

"I think we're supposed to clean up the broken china," he told Kristina. "I guess we're lucky he hasn't kicked us out! Are you all right?"

Kristina rubbed her eyes. "Yes. Fine. Thank you. I'm sorry. Sorry we argued."

"It wasn't anything," Julian said, embarrassed.

He was very careful not to look at Kristina in her underwear. He crawled under the bed, quick and catlike, to fetch her blouse.

*

When night fell, Kristina bolted the door and shuttered the window. The room was stuffy and smelled of pine; it was like being in a packing crate. Kristina lay head to foot alongside Julian and tossed and turned. She kicked off the suffocating bedspread and threw away the fat pillow. It was impossible to get comfortable, and she didn't dare to sleep.

After an hour or so, Julian got out of bed and opened the shutters to let in the cool night air. He climbed up to sit on the windowsill again.

"I'll keep a lookout," Julian told Kristina. "I can sleep in the plane tomorrow."

Kristina could see Julian's silhouette – black against the indigo sky, one knee bent, one hand holding his father's gun, just in case.

"You can't sit there all night!" Kristina objected.

"Watch me."

The shadowy profile of Julian's young head was alert and tense, his chin raised.

No one's going to tangle with that kid, Leopold's voice said in Kristina's head. *Go to sleep.*

The tiny cabin was cooler now that the window was open again, and the air smelled of sea and pine.

Kristina slept.

CHAPTER 20

The next day, Kristina flew most of the way across northern Italy in one long five-hour flight. She landed to refuel but wanted to keep going – it was only early afternoon, and she knew that the border with France was only about a hundred kilometres further. She could follow the Mediterranean coast now and didn't even need a map.

But Julian had his eye on her and hadn't missed how tired she was. They finished lugging the twenty-litre fuel cans back and forth from the local garage to the grass verge where the plane was parked. Then Julian pointed and said, "There's a stable."

The stable was a long, low building next to the garage, with an open front and stalls for animals. Two mules stood tied up in one of the stalls, peacefully munching on hay from an iron basket hung on the back wall. A rusty tractor was parked in the stall beside the mules. The other three stalls were empty.

"There's some of last night's bread and cheese left," Julian said. "And you can have the rest of that winter salami."

"Yes. All right," Kristina said. "We can do another French lesson." That would be a good way to use an afternoon of rest, she thought.

Kristina was struggling with the few phrases that Julian had taught her. She'd known the names of some French aircraft, but she didn't know anything about how to speak the language. The words Julian made her repeat didn't sound anything like the words she knew.

"Start with, 'Hello, my name is Kristina Tomiak. I am a Polish pilot,'" Julian suggested.

"Hello, my name is Kristina Tomiak. I am a Polish pilot," Kristina repeated. Her tongue struggled with the strangeness of it. None of it sounded right to her. "Why do you need the little word 'a'?" she asked. It wasn't something that was used in Polish.

"The French use more words than we do," Julian explained. "You have to follow their rules so you don't sound stupid. Just learn it! Hello, goodbye, thank you, excuse me, I'm sorry. Thank you and

I'm sorry are pretty much the most important things you can learn."

"We'll have to stop being Austrian and Russian when we get to France," Kristina said.

"Good," the boy said fiercely. "I hate being Austrian."

*

You're in France! Leopold told Kristina joyfully as she soared over the gleaming white beaches of the French Riviera the next morning. *What a beautiful day!*

Kristina's heart ached with loss and love. How proud Leopold would be that she'd made it here. How delighted he would have been to fly over this gorgeous coastline himself.

She finally forced herself to leave the beaches and fly inland, looking for a place to land.

And then, ahead of her, Kristina saw the wide green triangle and hangars of a French Air Force base. Neat little fighter planes were lined up at the edge of the airfield.

Her Polish plane was safe in France. She didn't need to hide in farmers' fields and orchard verges any more. She didn't need to try to pretend she was someone else.

There were two other planes lining up to land ahead of her. Kristina waited, circling overhead, until they had landed on the airfield and were safely out of her way. Then she too glided down to earth.

*

Excited airmen and ground crew came running out to meet Kristina's RWD-8. They waved and cheered, recognising the Polish checkerboard flag marking her plane. There was a roar of surprise when Kristina stood up in the cockpit and they realised that she was a young woman, not a man.

"Hello, my name is Kristina Tomiak," Kristina said, using the words that Julian had taught her. "I am a Polish pilot."

Nobody seemed to understand her attempt to greet them in French, but one of them turned out to speak a little Polish. He came forwards to hug Kristina and kiss her cheeks the moment she'd climbed out of the plane. "Welcome – welcome!"

Kristina felt as if she'd shrugged off a tremendous weight. It was a miracle that she'd made it here. She was among her own people again, in the company of pilots. Kristina felt as if she'd come home.

She glanced behind her to look at her passenger.

Julian hadn't moved. He was still sitting hunched in the rear cockpit, so low down that all Kristina could see was his dark, windblown hair standing up in tufts on his head.

"Julian, come down!" Kristina called in Polish. "These are friends."

Julian stood up in the cockpit. For once his face wasn't pale; for some reason he'd blushed very pink. Kristina wondered if he was embarrassed by her terrible French.

"Come down," Kristina repeated, and Julian had no choice but to climb out of the plane.

*

Kristina and Julian were given their evening meal in the officers' mess hall at the airbase. There was more food than either of them had seen in a month, and wine too. Julian sat pale faced and silent, picking at his dinner. He let the Polish-speaking French pilot do the translating for Kristina. Julian seemed to have shrunk – among all these uniformed men he looked even smaller, a weedy and unimportant little boy. He sat politely at Kristina's side, every inch the headmaster's son. Julian was clearly experienced at sitting through adult dinner conversation without misbehaving.

Kristina noticed that the muttered words of thanks or refusal that Julian gave in French were not the same responses he'd taught her to say. But she didn't have a chance to ask him about it while they were eating.

Afterwards, they were given a bare but comfortable guest room in the airbase headquarters with neatly made twin beds. Julian had to stay there by himself while Kristina was invited for cigarettes and cognac with the lieutenant-colonel, who was the commander of the base.

"You understand a little English?" the Polish-speaking French pilot asked Kristina as he lit a cigarette for her. She'd discovered his name was Antoine. "If so, you may not need me to translate the French for you. The commander speaks English."

"English? No, not at all," Kristina said. "Why ...?"

"But you spoke English at the table," Antoine said. "And you introduced yourself in English when you arrived. You said, 'Hello – I am a Polish pilot.'"

"That was *English*?"

It took Kristina a moment to understand.

Then she realised: England had always been Julian's goal. Every single thing he'd done since Kristina had met him had been calculated to get him to England. And like Julian, now Kristina was able to say hello and goodbye and thank you and I'm sorry, to ask for food and simple directions, and to tell people who she was in English.

Julian hadn't taught her a single word of French.

He'd coached her to speak in English.

CHAPTER 21

A surge of betrayal and anger slammed into Kristina at what Julian had done, filling her whole body. She dropped her cigarette and sat bent over with her elbows on her knees. Her forehead rested on her clenched fists, her eyes squeezed shut against outraged tears.

The sneaky, selfish little brat had taught her *English*.

At last Kristina raised her head and straightened her back, burning with embarrassment. She couldn't let these French Air Force officers know how stupid she'd been – how easily she'd let this sly kid fool her.

"Sorry, I'm exhausted," Kristina said as Antoine picked up her cigarette and gave it back.

The commander spoke, and Antoine translated his words. "We're the ones who should apologise. You've earned a good night's sleep. We can talk again in the morning, but I wanted to get a few things settled now to put your mind at rest for tonight."

Kristina nodded to show she'd understood, and the commander continued to speak.

"I've made a few telephone calls. We're expecting a Polish flight group to be created at Tours. We can transfer you there, and you can work in communications for the French Air Force until the other Polish pilots arrive. I've had our lads in the workshop give your plane a comprehensive service – you can fly to Tours yourself."

"Oh, thank you!" Kristina burst out, remembering what Julian had taught her, and then realised that she must be speaking English.

Kristina blushed, and the anger she felt towards Julian for tricking her surged through her again. It drowned out any relief and gratitude she felt. "I mean ..." Kristina turned to Antoine and asked, "How do you say 'thank you' in French?"

"*Merci. Merci beaucoup.*"

"*Merci beaucoup,*" Kristina repeated.

The commander smiled.

"I've made arrangements for the boy as well," he went on to tell her, again with Antoine translating for him. "There's an orphanage run by nuns not far from Montpellier, and the Sister in charge is Polish. It would be nice for Julian to have someone near who speaks a familiar language. He can stay there as long as necessary and he'll be well fed and given a good education—"

"Oh, but Julian has family in England!" Kristina couldn't help interrupting.

"I'm sure the Sisters will want to get in touch with his family," the commander assured her. "But the cross-Channel ferries have all been cancelled since the declaration of war, so he won't be able to go to England any time soon."

Kristina tried to imagine the determined, furious Julian Srebro settling down to the tight rule of a Roman Catholic orphanage. Another thought came to her.

"But he's *Jewish*," Kristina said.

Antoine put this to the commander, and they both laughed.

"The commander says, all God's children are lambs in the eye of the Lord," Antoine told Kristina.

*

Julian was still awake when Kristina got back to their room. He was sitting perched in the open window, just as he'd done in the tourist cabin in Italy, when he'd stayed awake all night long to guard Kristina while she slept.

"What did they say?" Julian asked.

"That I was speaking English, not French," Kristina answered coldly.

She sat down on her bed and looked at him. After a long moment of silence, Julian said in a small voice, "Sorry."

"You're *sorry*?" Kristina exclaimed. "You made a fool of me! You've been laughing behind my back the whole way across Europe!"

"No, I haven't!" Julian protested. "Laughing at you – are you crazy? I'm so in awe of you it makes me ashamed of myself! I wish I could be like you. I wish I was so clever that I could fly a plane and find my way over mountains when it all looks the same. I wish I could land in fields without panicking and fly through storms without being sick! And I'm scared of you sometimes too. I'm scared of you getting angry and I'm scared of you getting tired. But I never, *never* would make fun of you."

Julian took a deep breath. After a moment, he added, "But it doesn't really make any difference, does it? You'll learn French now. It was because I'm scared of you that I didn't tell you it was English. I wanted you to learn it so you could take me to England, but I didn't think you'd let me teach you if you knew."

"What a crazy, childish plan!" Kristina exclaimed. "You're just a selfish little boy."

Julian looked up at her. "I guess I am," he admitted. His eyes were full of tears.

And of course that was what he was. Kristina had more or less forgotten how young Julian was. Eleven years old, a sheltered schoolboy, whose parents were murdered just last week.

Kristina had to tell Julian the other thing she'd learned that evening.

"I'm going to join a Polish Air Force group at Tours. You'll have to stay here for a bit, and they've found a place for you in a ..." Kristina struggled for a better word than *orphanage*. "A children's home. Here in Montpellier. They'll help you get in touch with your family."

"I could get in touch with them myself," Julian said, leaping at the idea. "Perhaps the commander could let me use his telephone. You could ask him for me. I can take the train to Paris and then to London – there's another train that they put on a boat across the English Channel."

"I don't think you can travel on your father's passport without your father being with you," Kristina said. "And anyway, there isn't any boat. The ferries have all been cancelled."

She heard Julian give a small sigh of defeat and disappointment.

"You'll be safe here," Kristina said. "You can go to school. They'll feed you and give you new clothes. Probably get you special cream to take care of your eczema. It'll be better than a refugee camp, where you'd have no idea what will happen next."

Julian nodded. Then he climbed down from the windowsill and crawled into the other bed across from Kristina's. He turned his back on her under the covers.

"I guess I'll see you in the morning," Julian said steadily. "Before they take me away."

Kristina thought he was probably crying, but he hid it so well she couldn't be sure.

CHAPTER 22

Kristina lay awake in her comfortable, clean bed, unable to sleep.

Julian had sworn he'd never meant to make fun of her, and she believed him.

But in Kristina's imagination, *Leopold* was laughing his head off.

Best prank ever! Leopold cried joyfully. *Oh, come along, Kristina, surely you see the funny side – and now you speak a bit of English too! It might be useful! Didn't you even suspect? You must have suspected. You knew it didn't sound right.*

And then Leopold's voice said in a calmer tone, *Don't you feel sorry for the little guy, though? After tomorrow you'll have the Polish Air Force, but Julian will be completely on his own.*

Very softly, Leopold added, *Do you really believe the French nuns will be able to contact his family in England? The Polish Air Force will be all right without you for a while. The kid won't.*

"Julian?" Kristina said aloud.

He didn't answer.

She got up and stood by his bed, touching the lump where his shoulder was in the dark. Julian was breathing steadily and didn't stir or start. Kristina knew he was asleep, not sulking.

She moved the desk chair in silence, putting it in front of the door. That way he'd bump into it and make some noise if he tried to leave, waking her up. She was pretty sure Julian would try to run away from the Roman Catholic Sisters at the orphanage once he got there, and he might think of running away now to avoid going there at all.

Take him to England, Leopold's voice whispered in Kristina's head. *It's the right thing to do.*

She went back to bed, leaving the shutters open so the light would wake her.

*

Just before dawn, Kristina shook Julian awake and held a finger to her lips.

"Shh. Come on," Kristina said. "I want to leave early so I don't have to make excuses to a lot of people on the way out. I left a note. I don't think anyone will come after us – I'm not really doing anything wrong."

"What's going on?" Julian asked.

"I'm taking you to England," Kristina replied.

Julian didn't make a sound. No exclamation of thanks, no gasp of relief, no cry of hope. He sat up in bed, his face pale and drawn, and he re-knotted his school tie. He hadn't even taken off his blazer when he'd got into bed last night.

Kristina wondered if Julian didn't believe her – if his world had become so uncertain that there was no room in it any more for thanks or relief, or even hope.

"*Come on*, Julian, don't worry about your tie!" Kristina told him.

"It makes people take me seriously," Julian said. "People are nicer to tidy boys. And they're less suspicious of them."

Kristina's RWD-8 was standing outside one of the hangars of the airbase, wheels wedged, full of fuel, its engine freshly serviced. Her plane would never be in better shape for a flight across the English Channel.

She told the guards on duty that she was heading to her new flight unit at Tours and taking Julian as her translator. It wasn't entirely untrue.

It took them two more days of flying to cross France. Kristina stopped at French Air Force bases on both nights, in Bergerac and Nantes. On the third day, instead of continuing to Tours, Kristina flew to Cherbourg. The radio operator at Nantes had given her a proper aviation chart of northern France, including the English Channel and a sliver of the southern coast of England. The very last leg of the journey was from Cherbourg to Swanage in England.

The flight over the English Channel only took an hour, and the sky was quiet. But Kristina flew with her heart in her mouth the whole way. If something went wrong with the plane, there would be nowhere to land. For the first forty kilometres, she couldn't even see the coast of England ahead of her.

When she'd been flying over fields and forest and mountains, Kristina hadn't been able to see any boundaries of countries. But now that she was flying over the sea, she understood why Julian's father had felt his child would be safe in England. The sea was a defence all of its own.

Kristina's small, unarmed RWD-8 arrived safely over the cliffs of the south coast of England, and nobody tried to turn it away.

*

Julian hung up the telephone in the red-painted English telephone kiosk outside the railway station in Bournemouth. He stood for a moment by himself, then carefully rubbed his eyes with his chapped knuckles and opened the heavy kiosk door made of glass and iron. Julian stepped out to where Kristina was waiting for him.

"My aunt said I can't possibly stay with them in London," he announced carefully. "My aunt and uncle have just evacuated all their own children in case Hitler starts dropping bombs there. She was sobbing on the phone. But she said to come to London on the train anyway – and she and my uncle will arrange for me to be evacuated too."

Julian looked up at Kristina with a resigned, sad little half smile.

"So I guess that's what I'll do," he said. "Better than a refugee camp, anyway. Like you said."

"Will you go to the same place as your cousins?" Kristina asked.

"I don't think so. They're evacuating all the children in London, and it sounds like they just send you anywhere. To anybody in the country who says they'll take children in. My *cousins* didn't even get to stay together. My aunt was sobbing about that too."

"It's your war work," Kristina told Julian. "It doesn't matter how old you are – this is the work you have to do, and you're a soldier. You did exactly what your father ordered. And now you have to continue with the consequences."

"You will too," said Julian.

Kristina nodded, wondering what the future held. She would have to fly herself back to France. It seemed crazy to have come all this way to just turn around again, but for now, France was where her work was, and her people.

"So you'll get the next train to London?" Kristina asked Julian. He'd already bought a ticket.

"Yes. I have to change trains a couple of times, but I'll be there before it gets dark. My aunt will meet me," Julian said. "I'll get to see their house even if I don't get to stay there."

He gazed at Kristina with his calm, sharp green eyes. "I'll be all right," he said.

"Give me your aunt's address," Kristina said.

Julian got out his notebook and pen. He tore out a piece of paper, scribbled on it and gave it to Kristina.

Then he said shyly, "I have something else for you."

Julian held open his chapped fingers with his palm upwards.

On his hand lay a tarnished silver Polish Air Force pilot's badge: a white eagle almost exactly like the one Kristina had given to Leopold.

"It was my dad's," Julian said. "From the last war. But yours is gone, so you'd better have this one."

Kristina lifted the eagle from Julian's open hand.

With solemn pride, she hooked the pin onto her Air Force tunic, just above her heart.

"Thank you," Kristina said. She kissed Julian on the cheeks three times, just as she and Leopold would have done.

They heard the whistle of the train approaching. Julian crossed past the barrier. Kristina watched him go – a determined, neat and fierce figure, moving like a cat. His head was up and alert as he checked for the correct platform number.

Kristina had only known Julian for a week. Yet she felt like she was losing her best friend.

Julian turned and waved. And then he used Leopold's words without knowing he was doing it.

"*Stay safe!*" he called to her.

Kristina's heart swelled with love.

She'd fight for them both now.

AUTHOR'S NOTE

I was inspired to write *White Eagles* by the Polish pilot Anna Leska and her experiences in the Second World War. Anna qualified as a glider pilot when she was eighteen years old and then learned to fly balloons and powered aircraft. The Polish Air Force selected Anna to fly liaison missions for them when Nazi forces invaded Poland in September 1939. The airfield where she was working was taken over by the Nazis, so she took one of the planes stationed there and escaped in it.

Anna Leska rejoined the Polish Air Force in France. In May 1940, the Nazis also invaded France, and Anna made her way to Britain. In 1941, she joined Britain's Air Transport Auxiliary (ATA) and was able to do war work by relocating aircraft for the Royal Air Force.

Anna Leska was one of three Polish women who flew with the ATA during the war, along with Jadwiga Pilsudska and Barbara Wojtulanis. Anna became a flight leader in charge of an international group of female pilots from Britain, America, Argentina and Chile. I would have loved to end *White Eagles* with Kristina joining the ATA as Anna did, but it didn't fit in the tight timing of the story. Yet I like to think that after the end of the story, as the war progresses, Kristina will end up like Anna Leska – awarded medals by both Britain and Poland for her service in the air during the Second World War.

Anna Leska was one of thousands of Poles who fought against Nazi forces in France and then fled to Britain when France was also invaded. But most Polish soldiers and pilots didn't get to fly all the way across Europe in one week the way Kristina does in *White Eagles*. Many of them made their way to Britain very slowly after the Nazi invasion of Poland. For some people, it took a whole year to get there. They travelled on foot and by boat and by train, sometimes going the long way around via the Black Sea and the Mediterranean Sea. People even ended up passing across northern Africa as they tried to avoid being caught by the Nazis in Europe.

The Poles who had fled their country thought of Britain as "the Island of Last Hope". Polish pilots flew in the Battle of Britain with the Royal Air Force and even had their own squadron of Hurricane fighter aircraft. By the end of the Second World War, about two hundred thousand Poles had fought for their country while in exile in Britain. Over 19,000 of them served in the Polish Air Force or in Britain's Royal Air Force.

Kristina's journey is fictional and happens very fast, but I based the violent defeat of her Air Force unit and her desperate escape on facts. Kristina's experience is typical of the horror that many, many people had to deal with as the Nazis invaded Poland. The brutal treatment that Kristina's and Julian's families suffer at the hands of the enemy invaders is also created from true accounts. Hitler wanted to wipe out both the Polish nation and its culture – if he'd had his way, the entire Polish population would have been destroyed.

One of the horrifying operations Hitler used was called *Intelligenzaktion*, in which the Nazis secretly murdered about one hundred thousand educated and professional Poles. They targeted people like teachers, doctors, social workers and lawyers – anyone with more than a secondary-school education who might be likely to lead a resistance movement against the Nazis. The *Intelligenzaktion* executions took place a little later than the time at which *White Eagles* is set, and the Birky Language School is fictional. But real teachers were murdered as part of the *Intelligenzaktion* programme.

There was no happy ending for Poland after the Second World War. About six million Polish citizens, half of them Jewish, were killed during the war – about 20 per cent of its population. After the war, the Soviet Union took over the administration of Poland. The Soviet Union's influence was so strong that the British government barred Polish forces from participating in the London Victory Celebrations of 1946 because Britain didn't want to offend the Soviet Union. It didn't matter that every other Allied nation was represented at the celebrations. It wasn't until 1989 that Poland once again became an independent nation, fifty years after the Nazi invasion.

I have written many books that are set in the past, but I feel strongly that there is a direct link between then and now. Those people were *just like us*. When I'm writing, I try to include details that we can relate to in a personal way – like the chocolate coins that Julian shares with Kristina, and the man walking his dog in a Budapest park on a Sunday afternoon. There were refugee camps in Eastern Europe eighty years ago and there are refugee camps in Eastern Europe *right now*. We are connected to our past not just by our remembrance but also by our shared experiences.

It is important to remember how Britain welcomed citizens in exile from all over Europe during the Second World War, and how the Allied nations and the citizens of the Nazi-occupied European countries fought together gallantly to defeat Hitler's forces. These events are separated by time, but not by space. We walk on the same ground and fly across the same skies as those who fought in the Second World War.

Kristina and Julian both notice that you can't see national boundaries when you're flying over them. They also meet many different kinds of people in their journey across Europe – good and bad, kind and unkind, generous and selfish. Some people have strengths and flaws at the same time, like the flight commander who tries to take care of Julian by sending him to an orphanage where he probably won't be very happy.

Being flawed makes us human. Trying to overcome those flaws makes us heroic.

White Eagles is a snapshot of a past time and places that still have many connections to us in the present day. I hope you will find special connections here of your own.

Our books are tested
for children and young people by
children and young people.

Thanks to everyone who consulted on
a manuscript for their time and effort in
helping us to make our books better
for our readers.